I. Murderman

Manor House Publishing Inc.
(905) 648-2193

You're on my hit list
for calling me

Creep

I. Murderman

Manor House Publishing Inc.

Canadian Cataloguing
in Publication Data:
Murderman, I. , 1954-
You're on my hit list for calling me
Creep/I. Murderman
ISBN 0-9731956-4-9.
I. Title. PS8557.A8188C74 2002
C813'.6 C2002-905361-7
PR9199.4.M87C74 2002
First Edition. 96 pages.
Printed in Canada by Webcom Limited.
Published November 15, 2002
by Manor House Publishing
(905) 648-2193

Contents

Manor House Publishing Inc.
(905) 648-2193

Creep

I. Murderman

You knew

You knew
I'd find you
not far from where you live
not far from completion

You knew
I'd find you
and you knew that I'd give
my gift of completion

What you did
has bothered you
but soon your end will come
you will find completion

You knew
I'd find you
somewhere, someplace, sometime
you knew you'd have to die

Chapter One

Why you're reading this book

It's no accident that you're reading this book.

Nothing in this life ever happens by chance. There's a reason for everything.

You've picked up this book because you were meant to read it. This isn't chance. It's fate.

Most people walk right by this book. It

means nothing to them. But you were drawn to this book for a reason: It's all about me. And you. And the people I've killed. And the people I will kill, including you.

Don't think you can hand this book to someone else and have it mean anything. It's not them I want to kill. It's you.

Years ago, you laughed at me; you called me creep and looked down at me.

You, and the other scum, treated me badly and scarred me forever. All of you ruined my life.

Now, it's payback time.
Congratulations, you made my hit list.

In fact, you're one of the few people on my list that I haven't killed yet.

But you deserve to die and I've plenty of time to track you down and kill you.

I intend to do so soon.

And, thanks to the cash-upfront deal I signed with this shitty little publisher, I now also have enough money to live on while I come after you and my other remaining subjects.

Why Manor House Publishing?

The question should really be: Why not?

They're the only publisher that didn't turn

me down, that didn't reject my idea of a book based on my diary of past recollections, retributions and my completely justified killing campaign.

Manor House was the only one that didn't insist on meeting me and knowing my real name.

And they gave me a nice chunk of cash up front (but I won't be getting any royalties – I can't give them an address to send the money to).

The publisher asked me to write about my kills, about my life story in as much detail as I care to provide.

Apparently there's likely to be strong readership interest in all of this.

I'm told the public is pretty much always fascinated to get a chance to get inside the mind of killer and see what makes him tick, see if they can unravel the mystery in all this, see if they can figure out who I'll hit next and where I'll strike – define my hunting territory.

So this book is a hodge podge of stuff I've remembered, things burned into my memory, anecdotes, recollections, thoughts.

In revisiting my notes and memories I'm reliving the past.

And it only makes me more convinced

than ever that more people will have to die to atone for the wrong they did to me. I believe that deep down, they know they don't deserve to live.

You know you don't deserve life after your cruelty toward me.

I'm going to rip the life force from your body and leave your corpse on the ground.

Your departing spirit and I will stand together briefly and look at your body.

How will your body look lying on the ground? Peaceful? Grotesque?

You'll be complete and I'll move on to the next one on my list.

But I'm getting ahead of myself…

Obviously my name isn't really I. Murderman. That would be a little too easy for the cops, who have a nasty habit of getting close to me before I move on to my next subject. I have no desire to get caught.

Murderman is my pen name.

The publisher doesn't like it and suggested I go with I. Redrum since redrum is murder spelled backwards.

But the redrum thing has been done before – and I think Murderman gets the point across more effectively.

It's what I do. It's what I am.

And you're about to learn, personally, how good I am at killing.

I want you dead. I honestly can't wait for you to die.

Feeling a cold chill down your spine? Good. Get used to it. It'll soon get worse.

Despite the Murderman pen name, I don't consider myself a murderer.

I'm not just killing for the sake of killing. I have a true sense of purpose and legitimate reasons for taking lives.

With God's help, I'm bringing about long overdue justice. I'm making my half-formed subjects complete by settling old scores and righting past wrongs.

Only in death can you and the others regain the innocence you once had, before you indulged in your vicious treatment of me.

I'm performing long-overdue valid retributions, not senseless, cold-blooded murders.

In fact, I feel a great deal when I kill: Exhilaration, relief, and a rush of pure adrenalin. Sometimes, I've even felt some remorse.

But I know it's necessary that the past acts of my subjects and the subjects themselves be cleansed from existence.

And my mission continues.

You will soon come to realize that your lack of punishment for calling me creep and ridiculing me has left a void in your own life, an empty place in your soul.

I intend to fill that void. I intend to complete you by taking your life.

And I will. I have all the time and money and desire necessary to carry out this task.

More importantly, I have this book.

And I strongly suggest you read every word I've written.

It may save your life.

Maybe if you read this entire book, you'll get an understanding of how and why I've been pushed by people like you to kill again and again and again. And again.

And maybe you'll also get to know me and realize what a reasonable person I really am.

I hope you'll soon come to understand that my actions are nothing more than a very reasonable response to the way I've been treated. I'm actually pretty normal.

Maybe too, you'll be able to use this insightful knowledge to figure out who I am and what makes me tick.

Then, maybe you can figure out what to

say or do to save yourself and improve our relationship. And make no mistake: We do already have a relationship: Hunter and prey.

However, this basic relationship could possibly change and become more meaningful (and possibly a lot healthier for you) if you take the time to understand where I'm coming from.

I have to admit; I might have spared a couple of my tormenters – my subjects – had these people at least remembered me from school.

But, no sooner did I start feeling sorry for them than my sadness turned to rage. How could they not remember their nasty treatment of me?

Considering everything, how could they not even remember me at all?

How could they lie there, bleeding, dying, and just look at me when I asked them if they'd like to apologize for what they did?

Don't they have any sense of shame, of guilt, of remorse? What's wrong with them?

But you'll have an advantage over these dead people: Even if you don't know me now, you will by the time you finish reading this book.

That may give you enough crucial information to save yourself.

At the very least, if I do kill you, the experience will be a lot more meaningful for both of us.

You probably already have an idea of who I am. And by the time you finish reading this book, you may feel you know for sure.

It doesn't matter if you figure out my identity. The police will only laugh at you if you tell them your life is danger, and then hand them my book as evidence.

The funny thing is, your life really is in danger.

But by the time anyone takes you seriously, I'll be very, very close to where you live and the end of your life will be at hand. At my hand.

But don't expect me to come right out and tell you who I am.

Police in several jurisdictions are investigating some of my past retributions (cops call them murders), and I actually physically bumped into a cop at one of the retribution scenes.

Although I was able to easily talk my way out of it (I guess I don't look all that dangerous; I look pretty normal, average), I don't feel comfortable having the police so near to me, asking stupid questions, so I began moving around a lot.

Thanks to the advance cash I received from Manor House Publishing,

I have more than enough money to keep moving and stay one step ahead of the cops while I pursue my destiny and take the long overdue revenge I'm fully entitled to.

This revenge is necessary for myself and my subjects. I need it to regain lost self-esteem.

You and my other subjects need it to atone for past wrongs, and what could be nobler than you giving up your life to compensate for your evil past behaviour?

Sometimes I think the cops are going to suddenly see the big picture.

But most cops, like most people everywhere, are actually quite stupid. They can't patterns, killing strategies. They can't see the forest for the trees.

But sometimes the cops get close.

It's like they're right beside me sometimes, breathing my air, looking inside me.

But that's probably just a feeling. They don't know what's going on. Otherwise, they would have found me and stopped me a long time ago.

I'm not worried. I like to use a variety of methods for scoring each kill, so there's no pattern and the cops likely have no idea that my retributions are the work of one individual.

But while I'm not worried, I'm not going to make it easy for anyone to find me.

I expect you'll finally figure it all out when it's too late.

It's funny, I can actually picture you crossing the street and suddenly putting it all together and realizing who I am – only to find me standing in front of you, or behind you, with a knife or a sharpened screw driver or a gun. It's the last thing you'll ever see.

I've been watching you for some time now. For me, that's normal. I like to take my time before making the kill.

Sometimes I'll even endeavour to prime my subjects with phone calls or "chance" meetings to let them experience a steady build-up of terror before I complete them.

But maybe I won't have to complete you, after all.

Maybe you'll find something in this book that will reveal a way you can save yourself.

A grovelling apology won't be nearly enough. It won't do it.

But it's a start. I don't know what else

might make a difference. I don't know what might be enough to spare you from the fate of my other subjects.

But perhaps you'll be able to figure it out for yourself once you read my story.

You'll want to read quickly: I'm already in town – and I know where you live. I may even be watching you read this book right now.

We'll meet soon, I promise you.

My story is taken from entries in my diary, recollections, thoughts and anecdotes, experiences painfully burned forever in my memory.

These are my reflections on the things that shaped my life, made me who I am today.

Yes, my life of pain is laid out before you in the pages of this book.

I haven't included everything.

But there's enough in this book that you'll probably recognize both of us.

All I'm feeling right now is a gnawing hunger, an all-consuming, overwhelming desire to make you dead.

I know you better than you know yourself and I want to kill you so badly I can hardly even stand it.

You bring this out in me. And you know you do.

Or maybe you don't realize how much teasing and ridicule of a child can forever adversely affect their self-esteem, cause real and lasting damage to their psyche.

But ignorance of the implications of your actions is no excuse. At least it's not an excuse that will save your life.

You'll have to do much, much better than that.

You're going to have to figure out who I am and why I want to kill you.

Then you're going to have to try and figure out a way to stop me or find a way to get me to change my mind.

I'll be frank with you: You make me want to kill, and I am driven to be near you, to draw ever closer to you, to watch you more intently, to move in slowly and carefully for the kill.

I can almost taste your blood as it splatters against my mouth.

I hate it when that happens, but it always does when you work a knife or a sharpened screw driver at close quarters.

Can you imagine our meeting?

I can almost hear your partly muffled

screams, your rasping, dying gasps as the last breath of life leaves your collapsing body.

Maybe you'll find a way to save yourself.

Or you can die trying.

I don't really care one way or the other right now.

But if you're even the slightest bit interested in the slim possibility you may be able to save your own life, I suggest you keep reading…

Learning to kill

You take something living
Then you kill, make it dead
Yes, practice makes perfect
It's easy if you try

If you're not learning to kill
You may be learning to die
We all make choices
Help me to decide
If you should live or should die

Teacher has a lesson
What a thrill, what a thrill
Now I'm really learning
I'm learning how to kill

And now it's really easy
Doesn't bother me at all

Teacher has a lesson
What a thrill, what a thrill
Now I'm really learning
I'm learning how to kill

Chapter Two

Learning to kill

I'm 11, maybe 12 years old, and asleep in my bed when my dad slaps me hard on the back my head and tells me to get up. He's taking me hunting for the first time.

It's a bitterly cold late fall morning.

As we trudge outside, the fat man who hates me is waiting, leaning against his filthy, rusted-out pickup truck

The fat man is Arnie, Dad's friend. He's big and bearded and mean. He stayed at our place overnight, drinking beer and whiskey with Dad all night.

For a while last night, I had laid on my upstairs bedroom floor with my ear against the floor and I overheard some of their talk.

I heard things aren't going too well with Arnie's sales job selling industrial parts. He says maybe his wife – Punching Bag as he calls her – is right: Maybe he isn't a good salesman because he's destined for better things (like what?).

Arnie says Punching Bag went and said something that made him mad so he "went a few rounds with Punching Bag."

I've seen his wife a few times.

The last time I saw her, she looked like somebody really beat her up badly.

I was told she fell down the stairs.

She must do that a lot because every time I've seen her she's got black eyes and fat lips and sometimes broken bones.

And Mom's just as accident-prone: She's usually got a fat lip or a black eye or an injury of some kind.

I hear Dad tell Arnie that he shouldn't feel bad because Punching Bag had it coming to her.

Dad says sometimes my mom insists on arguing or being irritating and she ends up getting herself hurt because she just won't listen to him.

"She just has to push it," Dad says.

"She can't just shut-up for five minutes.

She just has to push things until she gets hurt, and you know, she's only got herself to blame," Dad tells Arnie.

"But they're all like that: Women are stupid bitches. You can't live with 'em. You can't kill 'em."

The stuff they were saying bothered me and I don't know why I listened as long as I did.

But after a while, I was too tired to listen to them anymore and I climbed back into my bed.

I don't think Dad and Arnie (this may or may not be his real name) got much sleep. I know I didn't…

And now Arnie's outside waiting for us. Even outside in the cold air, Arnie stinks of booze and urine and acrid, rancid body odour.

Arnie's hard, dark, pig-like little eyes glint with hatred.

He shakes his greasy hair in disgust and makes a crack about me being a little sissy boy, a sucky cry-baby.

Arnie tells me to get in the back and keep my mouth shut and stop looking like I'm about to cry.

Dad gets mad at me and says if it was up to me and mom, I'd be wearing make-up and skirts. Then he warns me not to cry if we shoot a deer.

If I cry he'll give me the back of his hand

across my face. I wish I was still in bed. Or at school. Or dead.

The late fall air is bone-chilling damp as we pile into Arnie's filthy old jeep with no heater and rust-soft floors with garbage partly covering up rust holes.

My breath fogs in the frigid pre-dawn air as I wrench open the only functioning back door and climb inside.

The smell of stale cigarettes, vinyl, gasoline, damp dog and garbage rushes through my frozen nose hairs as I climb stiffly into the icy interior.

The climbing motion tugs my flannel pyjama bottoms and causes them to become untucked from my work socks, exposing my skinny legs to the cold.

I quickly tuck the soft flannel into my socks and pull the cuffs of my jeans over them.

My breath is a frigid fog that makes it hard to see.

I avoid the holes in the floor but can see through the holes the gravel driveway visible beneath the truck.

Fraying duct tape covers numerous tears in the painfully cold vinyl seats.

My eyes ache from the cold and my finger

tips throb in pain as I sweep my hands across frost-covered vinyl seats.

The shards of frost sting like the dust of broken glass as I brush away frost and clear away garbage strewn over the back seat.

I quickly shuffle through piles of fast food wrappers, cardboard coffee cups and ketchup packages until I reach the end of the frigid bench seat.

A brutal cold stings my fingers as my fingernails scrape away some of the thick window frost so I can peer outside at rows of dreary, working-class homes.

I rub my hands on my knees. I ache from the cold. I ache to leave. I ache. I ache. I ache.

But there's no turning back.

These men, these killers, have decided I am to join them in hunting, in making a kill.

At this point in my childhood, I'm sure I had never killed any living thing beyond a mosquito or some other insect.

Truth is, for the longest time, I never really wanted to kill anything or anyone.

For me, the killer instinct isn't something I was born with.

Unless the urge to kill was always somewhere deep inside me. If that's true, other people helped me find this killer instinct and made it grow.

All I know for sure is that I acquired the primal urge to kill sometime after this hunting trip.

The truck shakes as Arnie starts it up and backs out of the driveway.

As we drive toward open country, I try to think of something else, I try to escape in daydreams, imagine being someplace else, anyplace else.

But the lurching truck keeps yanking me back to reality.

We've been driving for a really, really long time.

I straighten and bend my legs again. I rub my knees to try and get them warm.

The truck has no heater so the cold never leaves. It just keeps creeping through my clothes, into my skin. I'm cold to the bone.

It's light out now and not quite as cold. But I can't get warm again.

I listen a bit to Dad and Arnie talking to each other: It sounds like they don't have any hunting licences or permits of any kind.

But they're not going to let that stop them from hunting.

Dad and Arnie figure they might as well trespass on a farmer's property and go hunting there.

"We've got a God-given right to hunt, to provide for ourselves," Dad asserts, "so why the hell do we need all this legal mumbo-jumbo paperwork, licences and permits and whatnot?

Arnie nods in agreement: "It's just bullshit work for the pencil pushers in the government."

We suddenly pull into a field and tear toward some woods.

The truck is bumping and bouncing over the rough ground.

Constant jerking around from the truck is making me feel sick.

My head smacks against the door and the ceiling.

"Slow down," I say. A mistake.

Dad's ring cuts my lip and cracks against my teeth as he backhands me hard across the face.

Everything goes black for a second… then red… a muffled roaring sound…

"…and keep your fucking mouth shut – do you hear me?"

I nod, dabbing the blood from my mouth onto my jacket sleeve.

After pointing his finger at me and giving me a hard stare, Dad turns around and opens another beer.

A couple minutes later, the truck finally lurches to a stop.

We get out and step down onto the damp grassland.

The soft, spongy ground squelches as my left rubber boot sinks into it.

The ground water quickly finds the torn-split seam of my black rubber boots. Cold water absorbs through my sock and engulfs my foot.

I've got a soaker.

But I know better than to say anything about it.

The men are getting the rifles out, setting up.

Their camouflage jackets puff up a little from the breeze we're facing.

I'm told to sit on the ground and not move or make a sound.

A few feet away, I find a slight rise in the field that's only a little damp and I sit there and wait. And wait. And wait.

Arnie and Dad talk only a little in very low voices.

With the breeze blowing toward us, their words are carried on the breeze about 20 feet to where I'm sitting.

I can hear what they're saying. They're

talking about what a disappointment I am. How I'll never be a man…

Now they've pretty much stopped talking.

Every now and then I can hear a beer being opened. I can hear them drink and swallow…

And now there's no sound at all.

It's quiet for a long time.

"Arnie," my dad finally says, a sense of urgency in his deep, gravelly voice.

"I see her," Arnie answers.

"C'mere," Dad says to me, and I carefully crawl toward him…

I'm right beside him now.

"Look," Dad says, his finger stabbing forward to point at the forest edge. "See her?"

I start to shake my head 'no' when suddenly the deer stops blending in with the background. I see her now.

As the deer comes into view, I notice she's close to us, maybe a hundred feet away.

She's so beautiful, peaceful.

The deer has big liquid brown eyes, graceful body, soft-looking tan fur. A beautiful, gentle creation of God.

"See her?" Dad says again.

I nod, smiling. "I wish I had a camera," I whisper.

"Here," Dad says gripping my hand. He pushes my skinny, little 12-year-old finger around the trigger.

He pinches my finger against the trigger, pressing/pinching really, really hard.

"Squeeze, slowly," he says as he pinches my finger harder.

The trigger is cutting hard into my finger.

I grimace but suppress the urge to moan in pain.

It feels like the trigger is going to cut right through my finger, sever it from my hand. I bite my lip.

Then, suddenly the trigger gives, sliding back. A loud crack-bang, then a roar-echo as the rifle bangs hard against my shoulder and chest.

The deer suddenly stiffens with a jolt, then jerks forward in pain. She bleats a loud, drawn-out rasping 'Whaaaa' sound as she staggers forward.

There's blood coming out of her neck now, drenching and darkening her soft tan fur.

Her legs buckle as she lurches forward. And she collapses to the ground in pain.

She's still moving a little, her legs twitching as she lies on the ground dying.

"Bingo," Arnie says. "Right in the neck.

She should be dead in a couple of minutes."

As we walk toward the fallen deer, my eyes fill with tears and I retch and vomit uncontrollably.

This is wrong. This is a sin against God. It's unforgivable. Evil.

And it's just the beginning.

Life into garbage

When you take
something beautiful
and kill it
You turn it into garbage

Wen you show
contempt for the living
by killing
You create nothing; you waste

The more you waste
The more you kill
The easier it gets
To be a garbage man

Chapter Three

Off with her head

The other thing I remember about my first hunting trip was Arnie cutting off the deer's head…

Arnie's cutting, ripping into the neck, using his big knife with a jagged, saw-like blade.

I'm bent over, throwing up and crying. Dizzy. Everything's blurry.

Just as I straighten up again, Dad gives me a fast, hard back-hander across the face, slitting my lip, knocking me backwards.

The second back-hander is even harder. It knocks me to the ground. My nose is broken and bleeding profusely. I've bit right through my tongue. My mouth fills with blood.

"Now you've got something to cry about you pathetic little suck – I'm ashamed of you: Crying and puking like a little baby over a deer," dad says, waiting for me to get up so he can hit me again.

I stay on the ground, slowly spitting out blood and using a sleeve to dab and wipe the blood from my nose as dad glares at me in rage.

"I told you what would happen," Dad says angrily, raising his right foot and bringing it back to kick me.

But he's distracted by Arnie, who's cursing as he cuts and tugs at the deer's neck. "Give me a hand here," he shouts.

Dad looks in Arnie's direction, then back at me. "You're a mess," he tells me as he turns and starts walking toward Arnie. "Clean yourself up."

I pull myself up to a seated position and continue dabbing and wiping away at the blood.

My shirt sleeve becomes slippery as my fresh blood slides against the congealed blood on my sleeve from the previous back-hander in the truck.

My eyes are swelling shut.

But through the slits I can make out both men wrenching and tugging at the deer's ripped-open neck.

There's a liquid, rolling-crunching sound, a wet-muffled crack-snap. The deer's neck is broken now and Arnie is again sawing through muscle and bone with his knife while dad pulls back on the deer's head, which is now hanging off the side of its body.

Both men take off their jackets and continue cutting and pulling at the deer's head. They're both drenched in blood and sweat.

"Finally," Arnie says, as the deer's head is torn from its body. He wipes his knife blade on his pant leg.

As Arnie sheaths his knife, dad hoists the deer head onto his should and lugs it to the truck, grunt and panting from the weight of it.

Blood seeping from the deer's open neck splatters against the ground as dad walks, leaving a trail of blood splotches behind him.

The deer head is lifted and dumped in the rear box of the pickup truck.

Dad and Arnie get in the truck and I follow, glancing back at the animal's headless body.

I realize the body will be left behind to rot. We've killed one of God's beautiful creatures, taken her life for no reason and turned her into garbage.

I feel part of me, my soul, has died with the deer. I feel dead. I feel nothing.

Sitting in the back of the truck, I look at the men drinking beer in the front as we drive down the highway.

I'm as sick as they are.

My soul is as black and twisted as theirs. I'm one of them now.

And there's nothing I can do about it.

Arnie suddenly turns down a side road we haven't been on before. "Let's see if that old whore's at home today," he says.

"Sure," Dad agrees. Then he turns in his seat and jabs a finger hard into my chest. "And you," he tells me, "will keep your damn mouth shut."

A short time later, we pull up to a rundown, two-storey tarpaper house that seems to be leaning slightly to one side.

"Wait here," Dad tells me, as he and Arnie trudge up to the house.

A red-haired older woman wearing a lot of make-up and a nightie answers the door.

"Let's all have a drinkie," I hear her say in a raspy voice as she lets the men in.

I sit in the truck and wait for what seems like a very long time.

After a while, I get out and walk over to a weeping willow tree by the fence and take a piss.

Suddenly, I hear the house door open and as I turn around, I see Dad and Arnie leaving the house.

The red-haired woman waves a martini glass in their direction. "Come back anytime," she rasps, raising a cigarette to her bright red lips.

Arnie zips up his fly as Dad bounds over to the truck and slaps me hard on the back of my head. "What's that for?" I ask.

"That's for the next time you do something that pisses me off," he says.

Arnie laughs: "Sucky boy wasn't supposed to get out of the truck." He kicks me as I get back in the truck.

"You should've kicked him harder," Dad says. "Toughen him up the little sissy-boy."

"I'll kick him good and hard the next time," Arnie promises.

Back home, Arnie drops us off and heads to his place. He says he's hungry and Punching Bag had better have his dinner waiting for him "if the stupid bitch knows what's good for her."

Just before Arnie leaves, Dad takes the deer head from the back of pickup truck, hoists it onto his shoulder and carries down the basement stairs.

I follow him downstairs and look at the deer head that he's just placed on a table.

"I'm gonna get a taxidermist in to stuff it, then we'll probably hang it in the living room," he says in answer to my unspoken question.

Mom comes down the stairs a moment later. "So," she smiles, "how did my two hunters do on their trip?"

"You've got eyes, haven't you?" Dad replies, pointing at the deer head. "Where's my beer?"

"I'll get it right now," Mom says, then notices my face.

"How did he get black eyes?" she asks. "What happened to his nose? Is it broken? What happened to him?"

"Don't ask," Dad snaps, then adds: "Your son's a clumsy ass – now get me my beer!"

Mom starts up the first couple of basement steps, then stops for a second to ask: "What are we going to do with that... deer head?"

Dad bounds over to her, grabs her by the arm and pulls her back into the basement, berating her: "Four times now you're told to get me a beer. Are you completely stupid? Are you a total moron? Are you completely brain dead? How many times do I have tell you something?"

"I'll go get it right now," Mom says, trying to free her arm. She's starting to cry.

"Damn right you'll get me a beer!" dad says angrily. "But first we'll take care of your attitude problem."

"I'm sorry," Mom says, "I'll get..."

"Bullshit!" Dad interrupts, then points at me: "You," he says to me, "get out of my sight, you little creep. Now!"

I scramble up the basement stairs. Before I reach the top, I hear the sound of the table being knocked against the wall and possibly some slapping sounds that are largely drowned out by Mom crying out in pain while Dad berates her.

What can I do? I can't do anything. I'm only 12 at this point.

They're the grown-ups. They deal with things in their own relationship. I have to stay out of it.

Oh God! Now it's silent! What's happened?

I run back down the basement stairs and find mom getting up from the floor, gingerly touching her bleeding mouth.

Dad is standing beside her, glaring at her, white-knuckled fists raised.

Mom is crying and bleeding and she seems embarrassed to see me standing there.

"I tripped and fell," she says.

She does that a lot.

Repetition

Repetition dulls the senses
Marching soldiers
Practice drills
Marching soldiers
Practice kills

Repetition dulls the senses
Deadly action
Again, again
Unacceptable
Becomes routine

Repetition dulls the senses
Killing loses
Its moral sting
Killing loses
Everything

Repetition dulls the senses
Repetition dulls the senses
Repetition dulls the senses
Repetition dulls the senses
Repetition dulls the senses
Repetition dulls the senses
Repetition dulls the senses

Chapter 4

Again and Again

The deer head never was stuffed.

Dad said that it was a fine specimen and that if the taxidermists were any kind of real professionals, they'd stuff it for nothing or next to nothing.

But Dad found anyone he approached was "unbelievably selfish," and wanted to be well paid for their work.

In fact, the last taxidermist refused to even step inside our house.

By this point, the deer head was in a very advanced state of decay and stinking chunks of rotting flesh were now beginning to separate from the bones and fall off.

Our basement and the rest of our house was full of flies. The stench was strong enough to make you puke before you actually stepped inside the house.

Finally, Dad ordered Mom to put all the putrid flesh and maggots in garbage bags and spray the house with insecticide.

I thought we had only turned the body into garbage and had saved the deer's head for some purpose.

But I was wrong, we'd turned all of this once living, beautiful creature into garbage. At the time, the sheer, stupid waste of life really bothered me. But I was then still learning how to be an effective, relentless killer.

I also thought my crying and puking during my first hunting trip would have been enough to ensure I was never taken on a hunting trip again.

But once again I was wrong.

Dad seemed determined to "kill the boy" in me and turn me into a man like him and Arnie.

And so there were more hunting trips.

I learned to numb myself to the act of killing. I learned to feel no remorse, no regret as I killed again and again. And again.

The key to making these successful hits was in learning to develop a strong sense of remoteness, a sense of detachment that would remove me from the full and otherwise disturbing implications of the act of murder I was committing and remove the sense of regret associated with the corpses left behind to rot.

I can remember looking in the mirror as I was visualizing, imagining making another hit. My eyes looked dead.

I'd seen that dead-eyed look before and I was wondering where, when it suddenly hit me: I had seen in my own eyes, the eyes of a shark.

Surviving shark-attack victims often report that that as this massive creature moved in to bite them with its rows of jagged teeth, the creature looked like it was dead.

There would be no light reflected in the shark's eyes: They were a dull black that appeared lifeless.

Of course the closing of bone-crushing jaws on the victim's body is a reminder that the shark is still very much alive.

Yet the eyes look dead.

Like my eyes.

Part of the trick to all of this is de-sensitivity.

It's easier to kill if you can tune out the validity of the life before you, if you can deaden your mind, your eyes, to the enormity of taking a life: You reduce the living being to an inanimate object, a thing, a meaningless target.

Think of how soldiers were able to kill fellow humans in two world wars, the Korean War and the Vietnam War: The enemy was reduced to monsters, sub-human krauts, or yellow gooks that were just a half-step up from chimps.

It's also easier to kill an inferior life form, especially if you can make yourself believe that it is of no redeeming value to anyone.

You need to lie to yourself as I often lied to myself.

I justified killing deer on the pretext that they were a worthless pest to farmers, damaging crops.

Yeah, I was doing the world a favour by assassinating these gentle creatures.

Over time, I even grew to enjoy watching them die, when this previously bothered me. And I began to look forward to making each hit. Again and Again.

We didn't always go deer-hunting. We also hunted pheasant and ducks.

When hunting birds, Arnie's hunting dog Barney sat in the back with me (the seat always reeked of his damp dog smell whether he was present or not).

I wasn't allowed to pet this hunting dog, and he usually growled at me anyway whenever I sat next to him.

As we set about hunting, the men and I wore camouflage gear and concealed ourselves or tried to somehow sneak up on our prey.

Barney's job was to 'point' out the prey to us by silently betraying the position of fellow creatures who mistakenly did not take him for the deadly threat that he was to their lives.

It occasionally bothered me that this annoying hunting dog served no other purpose in life than to betray the positions of creatures who had just as much right to life as he did.

I detested this wretched dog, so eager to please his fat, obnoxious master.

Barney always looked so pleased with himself when he'd point out a group of hidden birds and in so doing guarantee their death.

Arnie and Dad would usually find an excuse to punch or kick me while berating me for being too slow getting them a beer or making too much noise.

I'm pretty sure they brought me along because of my high kill count.

But they usually made it sound as though if I wasn't there, they would have simply scored all the kills I normally made and not come home empty-handed.

In contrast to the way I was treated, the two men – especially Arnie – would be full of praise for Barney, giving him treats and encouragement every time the dog managed to point out some birds.

Barney would then sit there grinning while the birds were slaughtered and their carcasses left to rot (nobody wanted to pluck the feathers and gut them and prepare them for meals).

The dog actually seemed to enjoy setting up death sentences for the birds and then watching these fellow creatures die from steady deadly blasts of rifle fire.

Barney the betrayer.

Usually I didn't care that much. I found it a lot easier to kill birds than deer, which always seemed to be more majestic, noble creatures.

But there was this one time…

I'm with Dad and Arnie.

I'm around 14 years old. It's now sometime in the fall, before the geese have headed south.

Our hunting party is all outfitted in camouflage hunting outfits and hip-waders.

We're walking stealthily through fields and marshland looking for ducks and geese.

Dad decides we should fan out a bit to increase our chances of discovering some birds.

Barney stays close to his master Arnie.

But I start to experience a sense of freedom and I move well aware from the others and allow myself to lose my narrow killer focus.

I'm enjoying nature now, breathing in the fresh fall air, the crisp atmosphere.

I move very quietly, lifting my feet to make little impression on the land.

The breeze is blowing gently in my face. It feels good brushing against my skin.

The wet field gives way to marsh as I continue to move stealthily forward.

And then I see them: A beautiful mother Mallard Duck and her brood of newborn ducklings.

The mother is caring for her children, organizing them, protecting their little lives in a savage environment.

She loves these cute little ones who look to her for their nourishment, protection and survival.

I'm tempted to try to pick up one of the ducklings.

But I'm concerned it will only cause panic, leading them to fly off or draw some attention to themselves that could easily turn deadly.

I decide to carefully step back and move away. they need never know I was here.

As I take a few steps back, I suddenly feel Barney brushing by my leg.

He's headed straight for the ducks.

Out of the corner of my eye I see Dad and Arnie moving in, rifles raised.

I fire a shot in the air.

The ducks quickly scatter before Dad or Arnie can get a bead on them.

Now Dad and Arnie are moving in fast,

toward me. They're furious and cursing loudly.

They both start punching and kicking me and rapidly hitting me with their rifle butts.

"You moron!" Arnie shouts. "What did you do that for?"

"Stupid ass!" Dad shouts, knocking me to the ground with a shove.

I use my arms to try to deflect kicks aimed at my ribs.

But there are two attackers and a couple of Arnie's kicks connect with my lower ribs.

The two men stop when their energy and rage finally subsides.

As I rise to my feet, they're content to swat me with their hunting caps, throw the occasional punch and berate me.

"Stupid, stupid, stupid," Arnie says, suddenly sucker-punching me in the mouth.

"Good one," Dad congratulates him with a thumbs up sign.

I bend down and pick up my rifle as the two men turn and begin walking towards Arnie's truck.

I'm spitting out blood as I walk, my aching ribs making it painful to breathe.

Then, Arnie turns around and glares at me. "I ought to make you walk back you little shit –

what were you thinking?"

"Wellllllll," I drawl, forcing my mouth to form a bloody grin, as I notice Barney off to my right.

"It's like…" I add, still looking right at Arnie while I nonchalantly raise my rifle in line with where I know Barney is.

"…this." I pull the trigger and send a shell cracking into Barney's stupid skull.

The dog manages to yelp once before he falls to the ground and starts dying. I hope he takes his painful time.

"Noooo," Arnie wails. "Barney! Noooo."

Arnie rushes over to his dog and discovers he's well and truly dead now.

Now Arnie turns to me, his mouth drawn back in a snarl revealing scummy yellow teeth.

"Ooops," I shrug, still smiling.

"I'll kill you!" Arnie shouts as he starts towards me.

I raise my rifle, aiming right at him.

"Got one for you too," I say. I start squeezing the trigger. Arnie's face goes white. He knows he's about to die.

"Put the gun down," Dad orders. "That's enough from both of you. It was an accident."

"It wasn't an accident," Arnie says weakly.

"He meant to kill Barney."

"Your turn now," I say, squeezing the trigger harder. I can start to feel it give.

"Don't, don't," Arnie begs. "I won't do nothing to you. Don't kill me."

"It was an accident," Dad repeats, his voice shaking. "Please put the gun down. Nobody's gonna hurt anybody. Let's just go home now, okay?"

They're both terrified. Shaking. I can smell their fear, see it in their eyes.

I feel enormously strong, confident, powerful. Invincible.

And I keep the gun pointed at Arnie another few moments.

"Okay," I say calmly, lowering my rifle. "I made my point. Get in the truck. Now."

Arnie's hands shake on the wheel as he starts up his crappy pickup truck.

"That, that dog never hurt nobody," Arnie gulps as we pull onto the road.

Arnie's mouth draws back showing his yellow teeth and he sobs as Dad steadies the wheel.

I'm kneading my cracked ribs when I

notice Arnie's yellow-toothed expression of weeping grief.

And I have to smile through the pain of my aching ribs.

Someday, I promise myself, I'm going to kick those yellow teeth right down his fat throat.

We're continuing down the highway and we pass right by the side road to the old whore's house.

We won't be going there today.

I don't think either Arnie or Dad is in the mood.

Dad turns to look at me: "Maybe you can pass your rifle up to the front now," he says.

"Naw, that's okay," I answer, "I figure I might as well hang onto it until we get home."

This is the first time I've ever not done what Dad said. But he seems okay with my suggestion.

The rest of the ride home is in silence.

After we get home, I hand Dad the rifle.

He calmly tells me I won't be getting it back and he leaves the room and hides it somewhere. I never see it again.

Nothing at all is ever said about the hunting trip.

But the next day, Dad gets mad at me for something and punches me in the face and shoves me down the basement stairs.

I sprain my wrist protecting my cracked ribs in the fall.

Even though nothing permanently changed for the better, I'll never forget that hunting trip.

Come to think of it, that's also the last time I was ever invited to go hunting…

Things you say

The things you say
Can cut like knives
Into my soul

I am nothing
You've made that clear
You ask why I
even exist

But someday you will stumble
and fall and you'll make mistakes
that will tell me about you
and where you live; not why

I'm a loner
Worthless loser
And I'm waiting
To see you dead

Chapter 5

The new kid

We moved around a lot. No place ever really felt like home.

No sooner would we start to feel settled when we'd have to move again. I don't know why.

I do know Dad always complained about the management jerks at work.

It didn't seem to matter what job he had at the moment – there were always jerks bothering him at work and there were jerks at all of the jobs he had.

He'd quit or get fired and then find whatever job he went to had management jerks that didn't appreciate him and got on his nerves.

So we'd move again. And again. And again.

Because we moved around so much, I was always the new kid at school. And I got picked on. A lot.

People tell me that it's normal for a new kid at a school to get picked on.

Just because it's normal doesn't make it right.

I've heard that when a new boy comes into a new school, the other boys want to test him, see what he's made of, how much teasing and physical abuse he can take.

They say that's pretty normal.

Just because it's normal doesn't make it right.

I was on the small side as a kid.

Small for my age. Small-boned. A little frail maybe.

And I was shy. Painfully shy.

Maybe it as because of my home-life, but I didn't have much self-esteem or self-confidence.

I'd be quite happy fading into the background. I didn't want to stand out or make waves.

Most of all, I just wanted a friend, someone I could talk to, confide in.

A friend can make you feel good about yourself.

I think everybody needs at least one good friend.

But I couldn't get a friend. Nobody wants to be friends with the scrawny "creepy" new kid.

I just wanted to get along with people, have them ignore me, leave me alone and I'd leave them alone.

But people can't keep their hands and their big mouths to themselves. They have to bug. They have to tease. They have to hurt.

And, eventually, they have to pay.

When I started going to the same junior high school as you, I was hoping you'd be my friend.

But you rejected my friendship. Not blatantly and not right away: You started off being friendly. We talked a bit about school, music.

Then you started distancing yourself, looked the other way when I walked by.

Or you'd walk the other way.

You started cutting our conversations short. I'd barely get past hello.

And you avoided me. It hurt. A lot.

I was going through a lot at that time and I needed someone to talk to. Why weren't you that friend?

When I got beat up a few times – and I remember this really clearly – you just looked the other way. You tried to pretend it wasn't happening. You didn't want to get involved.

You couldn't even be bothered to ask if I was okay.

In fact, you couldn't find the time to give me any sympathy or spend any time at all with me.

It's like you just wrote me off.

Is any of this coming back to you now? Are you starting to remember things a little more clearly now?

You could have made a difference.

Instead, you joined the others in shunning me, isolating me and leaving me a target for ridicule.

I was alone in a strange school filled with strangers: Teachers and students I didn't know, whose names I couldn't always remember. I guess it really doesn't matter. You were all nobodies anyway. But you managed to stop me from achieving success by damaging my self-esteem.

Because I had so much on my mind, I couldn't focus on school.

I fell behind in my studies, got poor grades, despite the fact that my intellect is vastly superior to your own and that of the other students (and that of the teachers for that matter).

The poor marks would continue into high school and this plus my own poor self-image and lack of confidence – thanks again to the way you treated me – would later stop me ever getting a decent paying job or build a career of any kind.

My experience at school laid the foundations for a life of failure and disappointment.

What did I ever do to you and the others to deserve that?

My time at our school can best be described as absolutely miserable.

I was the butt of numerous practical jokes. My books were tampered with, pages glued together or torn out. My lunch was often thrown in the garbage so I went hungry most days.

You seemed to think it was pretty humorous when they'd pull my seat out from under me when I was about to sit down.

I'd painfully crack my back against the edge of the chair while everybody – including you – had a good laugh at my expense.

Frankly, I don't think any of this treatment was particularly funny. Certainly not to me and I think I've got a pretty good sense of humour.

Question: Isn't humour supposed to actually be funny?

I guess it must be a real knee-slapper when you hurt someone or throw their lunch in the garbage. Har har har. What a funny joke. You're about as funny as a rubber crutch.

Even if you didn't personally perform these various 'deeds' you helped make them happen by encouraging them by laughing and practically congratulating the jerks who tortured me.

But it didn't stop there: I'd try to ask a girl out and everyone would act like this was an incredibly amusing thing that was even funnier when the girl turned me down.

Why should this be such a huge source of amusement?

Are you and your friends completely brain-dead? (some of your friends are actually fully dead, brains and all – but that's another story for a later chapter in this book).

Like any normal guy, I wanted a girlfriend. Being shy it took a lot of courage on my part to ask a girl out.

I think I was rejected sometimes just because the girl didn't want to have to deal with all the rumours and people talking about how weird it would be if I ever had a girlfriend.

But what hurts the most was the nick-name I was given: "Creep." As if this single word somehow sums up everything about me.

A lot of people called me a creep, including you.

That's right, I heard you talking with your friends and you referred to me as being a creep.

Now you're on my Hit List for calling me "Creep."

Death of a salesman

You had trouble selling
industrial parts
to industrial customers

You had trouble selling
your body odour
to any normal customers

Better take it out
on your Punching Bag
Better go a round
with your Punching Bag

Now your Punching Bag
is leaving
Now your Punching Bag
Is long gone

Have you given any thought
to ending your sad life?
Your sales days are over
Sad death of a salesman

Chapter 6

Death of a salesman
and death of a nobody

Around the time I was having a lot of trouble in junior high school, I had some weird stuff to go through at home.

It all started when Dad came home one day with a surprise announcement…

We're seated at the dinner table when Dad tells Mom that Arnie's wife left him a week ago and it now looks like she isn't coming back.

"I don't know what's happened," Dad says in a disturbingly sincere-sounding voice. "They seemed to be fine. Now she's decided to embarrass him and check herself into a home for battered women. I don't know why. It's ridiculous."

Mom says nothing. As always. To say something, anything, would be interrupting.

And Dad has more to say: "I was talking to Arnie on the phone a little while ago and he sounded really down. Down and drunk. Plastered..."

I'm no longer listening. I've heard enough. This is fantastic: Arnie at home, alone and thoroughly drunk to the point of being incapacitated. Maybe even helpless. I have to get over to his house right away.

I excuse myself from the table to go to the washroom and instead toss on a jacket and head for an open window in the living room, making just one lightning-quick stop on the way to grab a nearly full bottle of whiskey from the liquor cabinet.

Getting on my bicycle, I go tearing over to Arnie's place, about seven blocks away.

I knock loudly on his front door. But there's no answer. The door's unlocked, so I quietly let myself in.

It takes a second or two for my eyes to adjust to the darkness. I look around. What a pigsty. All the drapes and curtains are drawn shut and all the doors and windows are closed, sealing in the stench of Arnie who hasn't bathed or brushed his teeth in years (it's true – he brags about it). Dirty dishes are piled everywhere.

Without making a sound, I enter the living room where I find Arnie, sitting on the couch.

He's sprawled out in filthy, beer-stained undershirt and track pants, feeling sorry for himself.

Arnie looks up and his beady little eyes narrow in rage.

"Am I shhheeing things?" he slurs. "Who let you in? Ged outta my house you little… pieshhha shhhhit… Ged out!"

"Looks like you could use a drink," I say calmly, holding up the bottle of whiskey.

"All my booze is gone, I drank all… where'd you get that?" he asks, noticing the bottle.

"I stole it from my dad's liquor cabinet," I answer truthfully.

"So this is your dad's booze? Good, I'll take it. Let's shhhteal sssomething of his. Good. Like he shhhtole sssomething of mine. Namely my wife… you know that?"

"No," I reply, genuinely surprised.

Arnie chugs back on the whiskey like it's a bottle of pop. "Isht true," he slurs. "Here's sah pishers," he adds, picking up a stack of photos from the coffee table and dropping them on the floor.

"I knew sssomething wash wrong, you know?" Arnie continues, "ssso I got a detective, you know? An' I got pishers."

I pick up the photos and put them back on the coffee table. They appear to have been taken at a motel of some kind.

"So your wife moved out? I ask.

Arnie takes another long slug of whiskey,

then nods his head. "Shhhhe moved – cuz when I found out… I, you know, boom, boom boom to her mouff and her fashe," he says moving his big fists around like he's boxing in slow motion.

"Sounds like she had it coming," I lie.

"Damn right," Arnie says. He chugs more whiskey. "You bring this?" he asks holding up the bottle.

"Yeah."

"You shhtole it right? From your dad."

"That's right."

"Good… You know your dad… and my wife… shhhlept togedder?"

"Yeah."

"Bastards… So what do you want?"

I clear my throat. "I need you to drive over to the beer store and pick up a case. I'll give you half the beer."

"I can't… drive," Arnie objects.

"You're fine," I lie. "I'll pay you twenty bucks for your trouble."

Arnie drains the last of the 40-ouncer. "Twenny bucks an' half da beer?"

"Yeah."

"Okay," Arnie says, rising unsteadily to his feet. "Lesh go."

I help the fat slob walk over to his home's attached garage, praying that he doesn't pass out before he gets in the pickup truck.

Just as we get inside, Arnie changes direction. His single-car garage door only opens manually and he decides he'll open it.

I'll get the door," I tell him. "Let's get you into the truck."

With my help and considerable effort, Arnie gets up and onto the driver's seat. He's starting to pass out. I unroll his driver's door window.

Then I put his keys in his pudgy fingers and turn on the ignition. The sound of his truck starting up briefly wakes him. "Door," he says.

"I'll get the door right now," I lie, walking towards it.

Arnie's head slumps down against the steering wheel. I leave the garage door closed and walk quickly and quietly through the side door into his house.

I wait around awhile, but the smell of exhaust fumes is starting to seep into the house. That's not good: If you breathe in a lot of exhaust fumes, the fumes can easily kill you by introducing deadly toxins into your bloodstream. That's an important safety tip.

So, I decide to leave through the front door. I get back on my bike and make my way back home. I really want to see Arnie again, later on. But I feel I shouldn't delay my return home any longer. Oh well, you can't always get what you want. Or so I thought.

As I walk back into the house, Dad is standing in the living room, looking pissed off. "You left without permission in the middle of dinner – where were you?" he demands.

"I went for a walk."

"Why?" he asks. Then his expression softens a little. "You upset about this business with Arnie?"

"Yeah," I reply. I quickly turn my back to him. I can't help it. I'm laughing silently but uncontrollably. My whole upper body is shaking with silent laughter.

"Well, don't cry about it – you're too sensitive," Dad says, then adds: "Listen, if you'd like, I'll be dropping off some sandwiches and smokes at Arnie's place and I'll maybe stay for a brief visit before my bowling game. You can come along if you want and I'll drop you off back here again when I get on my way to the bowling alley."

"Sure," I grin. "I'd like to see Arnie again."

As we pull up Arnie's driveway, I'm pleased to hear the pickup truck engine is still running. The body on the truck is in pretty bad, rusted-out condition. But mechanically, the truck is in fairly good shape. It runs well. And the engine can be left idling for quite a while without cutting out. It might not look like much, but it's a good, solid source of dependable transportation at a time when garage service charges have really become quite expensive.

Dad doesn't notice the noise from the truck at first and he knocks on the front door. There's no answer.

"I know he's home," Dad says. "Maybe we should just go in."

"Hey what's that sound?" I ask. "Is that Arnie's truck running inside the garage? Shouldn't he have the door open?"

"Oh my God!" Dad says. He races over to the garage door and wrenches it open. As he pushes it up to the top, exhaust fumes are billowing out of the previously sealed box-like structure.

Dad quickly yanks open the driver's door and checks Arnie for a pulse. There doesn't seem to be one.

"You wait right here – don't go in the garage – I'll get an ambulance," Dad shouts as he disappears inside the house.

I sweep away some of the pesky fumes with my hand and walk up to the garage to check out Arnie's fat corpse.

He's pretty much completely dead. Stone cold dead. Couldn't be deader. And he's got a stupid look on his face: He looks natural. What was once a worthless human being is now a worthless mound of garbage.

I'm fascinated by the look of Arnie's dead body. We've slaughtered a lot of animals but this is the dead human corpse I've seen.

Weird how things happen. You'd think a driver with his experience would know enough to open the garage door *before* starting the ignition.

But he was pretty drunk. He probably didn't know what he was doing.

I realize Arnie's no longer here. He's gone somewhere and left his body behind. He's just not here anymore. It's so strange being this close to dead guy.

It's also a little boring. I decide to join Dad in the house.

Dad cups a hand over the telephone when I walk into the kitchen. "I told you to stay put," he says. "Never mind," he adds, hanging up the phone. "We both might as well sit tight in the kitchen. The ambulance and police should be here soon."

"Have you still got those sandwiches?" I ask.

"Sandwiches?" he asks.

"The sandwiches you brought for Arnie. I'm feeling hungry. Aren't you?"

"Not really," Dad says. "But here, help yourself."

I've barely finished eating when the police and ambulance arrive one right after the other.

We go outside and show them the body.

The ambulance guys call in a body removal service and the cop – a big guy with red hair in his early 30s – suggests going inside where we can sit down and he'll take our statements.

"Why don't we make ourselves comfortable in here," the cop says, heading for the living room.

"Sure," Dad agrees. Dad and I sit on a couple of chairs while the cop parks himself on the couch behind the coffee table.

The cop pulls out his note pad and starts jotting down our statements as to how we discovered the body, what we saw, when we arrived, and so on.

Then the cop notices the pictures piled in a heap on the coffee table in front of him. As he goes to move them out of the way, he glances at a few of them. Then he looks at Dad. Then he looks at the pictures again. And then he looks at Dad again.

"This you?" the cop asks holding up a large print of Dad and Arnie's wife. They're both naked and laying on top of a motel bed.

Dad looks absolutely stunned. His mouth is wide open and his eyes are wide with fear.

"How 'bout this one?" the cop asks, holding up another photo of Dad and Arnie's wife having oral sex. "This is you too, right?

Dad nods, unable to speak.

"There must be twenty photos here," the cops says leafing through them, "and you're in all of them – is there something you'd like to tell me?"

Dad doesn't answer, so the cop continues: "I've been to this residence before – noise complaints, domestic disturbances and so on – and unless I'm mistaken, the woman in these photos is the wife of the deceased. Correct?"

"Yes," Dad finally answers. "But I have no idea where these photos came from. I've never seen them before. How did…"

"Given the existence of these photographs," the cop interrupts, "we're going to have consider this a death under suspicious circumstances, and we may want to bring you in for further questioning once I file my report, so stay close to home."

"Okay," Dad says weakly. "You think this is a suspicious death – you don't think it's a suicide?"

"Well at this point, we really don't know what we're dealing with," the cop replies. "But we can't ignore the existence of these photographs – which I'll be taking with me as evidence. Of course it could well turn out to be a suicide. But if that's the case, I guess you'd have to live with that too."

"Oh my God! You actually think I caused him to…"

"Oh no, of course not, sir," the cop interjects sarcastically. "I'm sure the deceased enjoyed looking at photographs of his wife cheating on him with his best friend at a sleazy motel. I'm sure that's why he had these photos laid out on his coffee table – for his viewing pleasure and convenience. I'm sure your conduct would have had nothing to do with him taking his own life… I'm just glad you're not a friend of mine."

I clear my throat and the cop suddenly remembers I'm also in the living room.

"I'm sorry you saw this, son," the cop says apologetically. "You were so quiet, I forgot you were here. Did you have a question?"

"Yeah," I say in an innocent voice, "how come Dad and Arnie's wife didn't have any clothes on?"

"You little creep!" Dad shouts, starting towards me. "I'll knock your teeth down your throat."

The cop steps between us. "You'll do no such thing sir." In his rush, Dad collides into the big cop, bounces off him and falls to the floor.

"In fact," the cop continues, "I'll be running a check on your residence and if I find any member of your family has sustained injuries at your hand, we'll be laying assault charges."

"I think my mom might have a black eye right now," I tell the cop. "Dad beats us up all the time."

"Somehow that doesn't surprise me," the cop says, shaking his head.

"This is bullshit!" Dad snaps as he rises to his feet in a rage, his fist tightly clenched.

"Bullshit?" the cop rejoins. "No sir, this isn't bullshit. You seem to be emotionally unstable sir and somewhat violent as well. We'll be taking you down to the station right now – no need to wait until I've made out my full report. We'll take your son home and we'll straighten you out at the station."

As we arrive home, the cop escorts me to the front door. Mom answers the door and her latest black eyes and fat lip are noticeable.

The cop then charges Dad with assault. Dad's taken away to spend at least tonight and maybe a lot longer in jail.

While Dad's away, I fill Mom in on everything.

At first she's completely shocked and she doesn't believe me.

But when I suggest contacting the cop for details, she realizes I'm telling the truth.

She offers to help me pack my things and we both move into a relative's home.

We don't tell Dad where we've moved. And we never see him again.

After Dad gets out of jail, he finds the cops are constantly questioning him about Arnie's death.

Dad goes back to our empty house and broods about his own wasted life and his role in Arnie's unfortunate suicide.

A few days later, Dad gets drunk and disconnects his brain with his rifle. He puts the barrel in his mouth and somehow figures out a way to pull the trigger. Or maybe someone comes by and helps him. I'd rather not say.

But I think most people took Dad's death as another unfortunate suicide, so we'll leave it at that. There's no point in dwelling on the past.

Only Dad and I know what happened and I consider it to be a private matter.

The weird thing is, after Dad kills himself, Mom goes nuts and checks herself into a mental institution.

And I'm bounced around from one relative to another, just as I'm entering high school.

Sorry

You've never said you're sorry
for all the things you did
You've never said your sorry
for messing up my life.

Now,
as your life
comes to an early end

Now,
as you pray
that I'll never find you

You regret your bad deeds
that ruined my young life.
You'd like to say you're sorry
for leading me astray

Yet,
you're dying now
even now, as I speak.

Chapter 7

You make me want to kill you

When I caught up with you in high school, I probably seemed a little more confident in myself.

Unfortunately it wouldn't last.

I was told everything would be different in high school: The school drew in kids from all over, so in essence, everyone in Grade 9 is a "new kid."

There was also supposed to be a lot more freedom and responsibility in high school. You and I got to choose our own courses, pursue our own areas of study, chase our own dreams.

Gone were the days when you could end up in a class full of kids who'd spent their whole lives up to that point sharing the same classes. In that scenario, the newcomer sticks out like a sore thumb.

For the most part, the things we'd both heard about high school were true.

But high school wasn't the "great equalizer" it was billed as.

No, I was a stranger in a sea of strangers, I found there were a good many of my former junior high classmates attending many of my high school classes.

And with these classmates came the same little cliques, the same nasty rumours, the same "creep" nickname I hated.

Once again, you started off the school year being friendly with me. Then, once again, you kept your distance when the others made it clear I was still "uncool," a geek, a creep you didn't want to be seen with.

At this point in my life, I'd lost my father to suicide and my mother to mental illness. I was moving back and forth from relative to relative – whoever drew the short straw got the kid nobody wanted.

I didn't even like most of these people. And I know they didn't like me. Most of them couldn't be bothered packing me a lunch and wouldn't think of giving me lunch money, so most days I went hungry through the lunch break.

I was also ridiculed for wearing the same out-of-fashion pants and shirt day after day. There's a reason for that: It's all I had to wear.

The people I was staying with wouldn't dream of buying me a pair of jeans, not when they could hand me a pair of ill-fitting 1950s era trousers they wouldn't be caught dead in themselves.

And the people I was staying with – family is too strong a term, they were nothing more than reluctant relatives who were meeting obligations they'd much rather have ignored – also played havoc with my social life, setting 7:30 pm curfews on weeknights, organizing mandatory "family picnics on Saturdays and church outings on Sundays. With these kinds of constraints it's next to impossible to forge a meaningful friendship with anyone. But I felt it was at least worth making an effort – it's unfortunate you didn't feel the same way.

I put up with the funny clothes, the ridiculous lifestyle, because these people also offered me something I desperately needed at that stage I my young life: Stability.

With these people, you knew where you stood. And, as long as you made the curfew on time, helped with the household chores and didn't cause problems, you'd have a roof over your head and dinner on the table.

I can't begin to tell you how much a sense

of stability meant to me after losing both my parents and feeling a deepening sense of isolation from everyone else.

I'd gone through a lot and I needed a friend. Again, you appeared at first to be there as a friend. But when the chips were down, you bolted, as always.

For the most part, I just tried to keep to myself and take a low-key approach to striking up conversations and making friends, usually with very little success.

I guess I was hoping people would eventually see through my goofy clothes and restrictive lifestyle and notice that I'm not such a bad guy.

But I have very different memories…

I'm standing in line in the cafeteria. I've got just enough cash for a small milk and an inexpensive plate of spaghetti.

People behind me are talking about me. But I'm almost used to that. It happens a lot. Yet, this talk is persistent and secretive. I'm getting concerning that something wrong is about to happen.

And it does.

One oaf of jock grabs my pants while his buddy dumps the hot spaghetti down my crotch. He then wipes the plate against my shirt and trips me, sending me sprawling into a stack of trays.

"Wait, wait," the first jock laughs. "We

need the crowning touch." With that, he grabs a bowl of hot spaghetti sauce and dumps it on my head as I'm struggling to get back on my feet. At least 50 people, maybe more, applaud, whistle, laugh and jeer at me.

I couldn't make out everybody in the cafeteria, but you were there. You were one of the people laughing and applauding.

The humiliation and embarrassment sting. I can't stop the tears welling into my eyes

"Nice pants creep!" says a girl I've never met.

"Hey," the first jock says, "he's not just a creep – he's the king of the creeps."

This prompts another round of jeering and name-calling.

The cafeteria lady has seen everything but said nothing, until now: "I hope you realize you'll have to pay for that spaghetti – we're not running a charity here."

I can't believe what I'm hearing. "I'm not… paying for this," I stammer.

"Yes you are," the woman insists. "If you're going to play around with food…"

"Are you blind?" I snap. "Did you not see them dumping food on…"

"If you're going to play with food you'll have to pay for it," she repeats.

"You stupid, fat cow!" I shout.

This prompts the jocks to play hero.

"Nobody gets away with calling Mrs.

Smith names you little creep," the second Jock says.

They take turns punching me while Mrs. Smith reports my unruly conduct to the office.

I get a three day suspension. I wish I could be suspended forever.

Another time…

I'm again in a cafeteria, this time seated at a table. I'm about to start in on a hot hamburger special when a jock wanders by, slides his hand under my plate, raises it and then turns it over and smacks it face down onto the table. He then smears it all around before sliding it into my lap.

As the plate falls to the floor and breaks, the jock stretches his arms to indicate how wonderful he is. He then takes several exaggerated bows while everyone in the cafeteria – including you – laughs and jeers and treats this act of humiliation as though it's some form of high entertainment.

Only one girl isn't laughing. Her name is Cathy and she apologizes for the behaviour of the jock, John (this may or may not be their real names).

She asks me if I'm okay and we chat a bit while John glares at us.

A few days later, I see Cathy in a school hallway. Summoning up all my courage, I ask her if she'd like to see a movie with me.

"Pardon?" she says.

It's noisy in the hallway, so I ask her again, a little louder.

"Oh my God!" Cathy shouts. "I don't believe this! Hey everyone: The creep just asked me out on a date!

Her announcement gets the hallway mob chanting: "Kill the creep! Kill the creep1!" A couple of jocks make a point of sucker-punching me in the back as they walk past me.

"Can you believe this?" Cathy says loudly, turning her attention to me. "What the hell makes you think I'd ever want to be seen with a creep-geek like you? Are you a total moron?"

"I'm… sorry," I manage. The apology adds to the humiliation. But I don't know what to say.

"You're sorry, you're sorry," Cathy repeats. "I should hope you're sorry. Yuck! Puke! I feel dirty. I'm gonna go home and have a shower – and you're not invited creep, so get that idea out of your stupid head right now. What girl in her right mind would ever want to be seen in public with you? Oh my God! It's so insulting. Get away from me creep before I smash your face in!"

When I leave the school that day, John is waiting outside for me.

Without saying anything, John starts punching and kicking me while a mob of his friends jeer and throw punches of their own.

They finally knock me to the ground and kick me until they grow tired of kicking.

Then they walk away. But John walks back to me for a moment, leans down and says: "Just one thing, creep: You go near my girlfriend again, ever, and I'll kill you."

The word "kill" seemed to echo in my ear long after the mob walked away. The word kill has a comforting sound and I let that sound wash through the deepest recesses of my subconscious. I knew that killing can solve problems and create a sense of power and I was really beginning to feel that it was tie to kill again.

Oh yeah, I found out later that John and Cathy had been boyfriend and girlfriend for several weeks. Cathy had been angry at John for flirting with another girl when she talked to me that day in the cafeteria. She pretended to be my friend to make him jealous. Oh well, I guess it was worth it. Someday, I'm really going to enjoy making them both dead.

Chapter 8

Why you have to die

Let's flash forward quite a few years...

I'm standing in the midst of woods on a late summer day. I'm wearing an old pair of dark blue track pants and a ratty old hooded sweatshirt, with the hood casting a shadow over my face, concealing my features.

I know I'm dressed pretty grungy, but I'm expecting my work to get messy. I brought a steak knife from home, and as I stand there in the woods, I run my thumb very lightly over the sharp serrated edge.

And I think about how I came to be in these woods on this fine summer day.

It took a long time, years in fact, for me to realize that the real reason, the root cause reason, why I keep getting fired from jobs and never seem to get anywhere has to do with the way I was treated when I was younger.

To say the way I was treated shattered my self-confidence doesn't even begin to say what needs to be said: I never even got a chance to develop self-confidence or self-esteem in the first place.

I've gone through my whole life believing I could never, ever be better than second-best – and that this would be a big step up because normally I'm the worst. I'm the guy who also comes in last at everything.

I remember one boss feeling sorry for me as he fired me. He told me that everything about me suggested failure. That even my body language showed a complete lack of self-esteem. And it's true: I'm like a dog that's been kicked so many times I walk with a permanent limp.

This boss – ex-boss – said even the way I walked showed a total lack of pride. My appearance sent out a message of poverty not just in monetary terms, but a poverty of spirit, an attitude of failure.

He asked me if there was something that had happened to me a long time ago that might have made me give up so easily on ever achieving any form of success in life.

And that's when I realized that all my

efforts to forget the past, to put it behind me, have never worked. What happened to me years ago still scars me, still shapes who I am, still limits me and confines me to one abject failure after another.

What happened to me – and it was many humiliating incidents, not just one or two – was simply wrong. I should never have been treated that way.

But the years of abuse broke my spirit and caused me to stop believing in myself. The abuse taught me that I was worthless and deserving of nothing more than a life of failure and disappointment.

It's not just jobs that I've lost. I've also lost every relationship I've ever had. I don't feel good about myself – why should anyone else? I honestly don't see any value in myself, I don't see any redeeming traits. I only see a loser. Why would anyone else see anything different?

I long to be made whole again.

And believe me when I tell you that recognizing the problem doesn't solve it: The sense of failure, the loser traits I've just described are ingrained in my personality and psyche. They're part of me. I hate myself.

I want to change this. I've tried forgetting the past, pretending it doesn't matter.

But it's not enough. I need to make the past right. I need to correct the wrongs done to me and make the perpetrators pay. That's how I'll recover my self-esteem.

I wander through the woods closer to the road, tapping the steak knife blade against my pant leg.

A rush of adrenaline is sweeping through me. I feel good. Powerful.

I'm waiting for someone special. She's a pretty blonde woman who always jogs along this road at the same time of the morning. She'll be here soon. Her name is Cathy.

Listen. There's a soft sound of running shoes hitting asphalt. Cathy's coming.

There she is. She'll stop at the stop sign and jog on the spot for a minute. She always does that.

Just as Cathy stops, I grab her by the hair and pull her down hard into the thick bushes right beside the stop sign.

I ram my gloved left hand into her mouth to silence her. The bitch is biting me as hard as she can.

My right hand rips the steak knife into her neck, ripping through her main artery. There's a huge amount of blood as I stab her again and again. She's not biting me now. She's dead.

As I run back into the woods, A searing hot pain radiates through my right hand. I stop and dab a tissue on it and find it's torn up like hamburger meat: The knife bade had been slipping up and into my closed hand. I resolve to use a knife with a hilt on the next time. I can't believe I was so stupid…

Now, I'm standing at a bus stop. An older woman approaches the stop, just like she always does. This is the bus that takes her to our old high school. She works in the cafeteria.

She always arrives at the bus stop early to give herself a little extra time to make the bus. It's all the time I need.

I walk up the street and then nonchalantly turn around and walk back toward her. I'm wearing a hooded sweatshirt and gripping a hammer in my right hand.

Just as I'm about to pass her, I swing the hammer fast and crack her skull open. It happens so fast, I'm sure nobody would realize what happened even if they were standing right there.

By the time she hits the pavement, I've already passed her and I'm a good 20 feet down the block. I don't even look back…

I use a hammer, or crowbar or a metal bar or a sharpened screwdriver or a knife – with a hilt – on about 20 other people. I call them the "laughers." They're the ones – like you – who may not have performed an actual act of humiliation, but still managed to add to the "richness" of the experience by laughing away. Don't underestimate the importance of yourself and the other laughers:

Without your laughter, your applause and encouragement, the jocks (they're mostly dead now by the way) might have lost interest and behaved themselves.

In fact, let's take it a step further: Let's imagine you and the other laughers had not only withheld your applause but made remarks pointing out how juvenile the jocks were behaving.

Yes, if you'd actually showed your displeasure, I'm sure that the act of picking on an undersized kid would have lost it s natural fascination for athletic goons who move their lips when they look at pictures.

Simply put, without you and the other laughers there would be no adoring audience – and therefore no show. Give yourself a pat on the back. You made the relentless abuse happen. The abusers couldn't have done it without you. Take a bow.

So don't sell yourself short. You're very much a vital and integral part of the problem and your timely death will be an important part of the solution. We'll meet soon enough…

I'm sitting at the window of an apartment now. I don't know whose apartment this is. I broke in about 15 minutes ago. I'm not here to steal anything. It's just that when I aim my rifle scope through the window, I get an unobstructed bead on a very successful businessman. His name is John.

I'm waiting for him to leave his home for work. He lives in a big executive home, but he's one of these people who uses their two-car garage as something other than a place to park your car. He takes 20 seconds to walk from his front door to the car in his driveway, and another 20 seconds to unlock the door and get inside.

I decide to use the rifle because I had a bad experience trying to complete a jock with a hammer blow to the head: The sonofabitch moved and the hammer only struck a glancing blow. Fortunately he was stunned enough that I was able to get in a much better blow. But it was close. I really don't want to get in a fist-fight with someone who's a lot bigger than me.

So, while I prefer close quarters so I can watch my subjects die, I'm pragmatic enough to recognize a rifle is the preferred instrument of choice when dealing with larger people.

There's John now. My shark eye turns him into an object, a slow moving target. I wait until he reaches the car and stands relatively still while he attempts to fish the keys out of his pocket.

I squeeze the trigger. The bullet smacks away a chunk of the back of his head ala JFK. For a second he just stands there. It actually looks like he's going to get in his car and drive. But then he collapses to the ground. Another problem efficiently solved.

I've already concealed the rifle. I'm now just another person who heard a gunshot and looked out their window. Even so, I pack up fast and slowly walk out of the building…

I'm in a shopping mall now, in a department store, pretending to look over some CDs while I watch my next subject intently.

You won't believe who I'm watching: It's YOU!

Congratulations. You've moved up on my hit list. You're ready for the big time, that one big final moment.

I'll be honest though, watching you is a drag. But I'll resume watching…

You're looking at a CD now. Now you're picking it up as though you're going to buy it. Now you're putting it back. Now you're looking at another CD and another. You're beginning to bore me.

I almost had you in the mall parking lot. But there were too many people around.

If you're wondering, I'll likely use a sharpened screwdriver. I'm also carrying a pair of pliers. That way if I'm questioned by the cops, they'll think I'm some kind of handy man. Clever, no?

Do you remember I indicated early in this book that you may find some way to save yourself. I may have been less than honest.

But let's face it, if I told you was going to kill you no matter what, you might not want to read the rest of the book. You might decide to move instead, and it took me quite a while to find you this time.

Then again, perhaps you haven't taken any of this seriously. That would be a BIG error on your part.

Make no mistake, I'm moving relentlessly down my hit list, crossing off each subject that achieves completion.

There are now very few of you left.

I did consider sparing you: Your involvement could be seen as being somewhat on the fringe rather than a core part of the abuse problem.

I carefully weighed your involvement and gave the matter careful consideration.

And I reached a firm conclusion:

You're next.

Manor House Publishing
(905) 648-2193